For Dr. Stephen Litwin, my father,
who told me my first stories
—E.L.

To Kim, the girl who told me she wanted to live in a small
cabin and make things out of clay
—J.D.

Pete the Cat: Rocking in My School Shoes
Copyright © 1999 by James Dean (for the character of Pete the Cat)
Copyright © 2011 by James Dean and Eric Litwin
All rights reserved. Printed in the United States of America.
No part of this book may be used or reproduced in any manner whatsoever without written permission except in the
case of brief quotations embodied in critical articles and reviews.
For information address HarperCollins Children's Books, a division of HarperCollins Publishers,
10 East 53rd Street, New York, NY 10022.
www.harpercollinschildrens.com

Library of Congress Cataloging-in-Publication Data
Litwin, Eric.
    Rocking in my school shoes / story by Eric Litwin (aka Mr. Eric) ; art by James Dean.— 1st ed.
        p.   cm. — (Pete the cat)
    Summary: Pete the cat wears his school shoes while visiting the library, the lunchroom, the playground, and
more while singing his special song.
    ISBN 978-0-06-191024-1 (trade bdg.) — ISBN 978-0-06-191025-8 (lib. bdg.)
    [1. Stories in rhyme. 2. Schools—Fiction. 3. Cats—Fiction. 4. Shoes—Fiction. 5. Singing— Fiction.] I.
Dean, James, ill. II. Title.
PZ8.3.L7387Roc 2011   2009053455
[E]—dc22   CIP
                                                                                                     AC

Typography by Jeanne L. Hogle
13 14 15 LP 10 9
❖
First Edition

Pete the Cat

Rocking in My School Shoes

created & illustrated
by James Dean

story by
Eric Litwin

HARPER
An Imprint of HarperCollins Publishers

Here comes Pete
strolling down the street,
rocking red shoes
on his four furry feet.

Pete is going to school,
and he sings this song:

"I'm rocking in my **school** shoes,

I'm rocking in my **school** shoes,

I'm rocking in my **school** shoes."

Pete is sitting at his desk when his teacher says,
"Come on, Pete,
down that hall
to a room with books
on every wall."

Pete has never been to the library before!

Does Pete worry?
Goodness, no!

He finds his favorite book
and sings his song:

"I'm reading in my **school** shoes,

I'm reading in my **school** shoes,

I'm reading in my **school** shoes."

Check out Pete.
He's ready to eat
in a big, noisy room
with tables and seats.

Where is Pete?

The lunchroom!

It can be loud and busy in the lunchroom.

Does Pete worry?
Goodness, no!

He sits down with his friends
and sings his song:

"I'm eating in my **school** shoes,

I'm eating in my school shoes,

I'm eating in my school shoes."

Pete and his friends
　　are playing outside
　　　　on a green, grassy field
　　　　　　with swings and tall slides.

Where is Pete?

The playground!

Kids are running in every direction!

Does Pete worry?
Goodness, no!

He slides, and swings, and sings his song:

"I'm playing in my school shoes,

I'm playing in my school shoes,

I'm playing in my school shoes."

All day long Pete sings his song.

"I'm singing in my
school shoes,

I'm painting in my
school shoes,

I'm adding in my **school** shoes,

I'm writing in my
school shoes."

When school is done, Pete rides the bus home.

"I was rocking in my **school** shoes,

I was rocking in my **school** shoes,

I was rocking in my **school** shoes.

And I will do it again tomorrow!

Because it's all good."

CLASSROOM 123